THE BOOK OF RUTH

A DEVOTIONAL STUDY

CHARLES LEE HOLLAND, JR

Copyright © 2020 by Charles Lee Holland

All rights reserved. This book or any portion thereof may not be reproduced or transmitted in any form or manner, electronic or mechanical, including photocopying, recording, or by any information storage or retrieval system, without the express written permission of the copyright owner except for the use of brief quotations in a book review or other noncommercial uses permitted by copyright law.

Printed in the United States of America

Library of Congress Control Number:	2020908972
ISBN: Softcover	978-1-64908-189-6
eBook	978-1-64908-188-9

Republished by: PageTurner Press and Media LLC
Publication Date: 08/12/2020

To order copies of this book, contact:

PageTurner Press and Media
Phone: 1-888-447-9651
order@pageturner.us
www.pageturner.us

CONTENTS

INTRODUCTION 1

CHAPTER ONE – THE JOURNEY TO MOAB 5

CHAPTER TWO – GLEANING IN THE FIELDS 21

CHAPTER THREE – RUTH AND BOAZ AND THE NIGHT AT THE THRESHING FLOOR 33

CHAPTER FOUR – THE MARRIAGE OF BOAZ AND RUTH 41

FOR OUR GRANDCHILDREN

Grady, Jonathan　　　　Holly, Heather

Megan and Matt
Hannah and Holden
Jeremy and Adrianne
Lacey and Mark
Lauren and Alex

THE BOOK OF RUTH
A Devotional Study

INTRODUCTION

This diminutive narrative is one of the greatest short stories ever written, and it is one of the most beautiful as well. It is quite simple in structure, but it is presented in a most appealing manner. The story is set in the ancient time of the Judges and involves a group of individuals who are destined to share an integral role in the ancestry of King David.

The principal character in the book is a Moabite woman named Ruth. The hero of the story is Boaz. The son of Boaz and Ruth becomes the grandfather of King David. The probable date of the events recorded is approximately the twelfth century B.C. As is often the case in the Old Testament, the books are named after the author. This is not true in the instance of the Book of Ruth. The book is named for its principal character. Some older commentaries suggest that the author of the book was Samuel. However, there is nothing in the book to indicate that such is the case. Neither is there any known external evidence to authenticate the theory. Thus, it may be said that the author of the book remains unknown.

So much for the setting of the story. What may be known regarding the actual time of the writing of the book? Well, frankly speaking, not as much is known as we might wish. In evaluating extant internal and external evidence available, most scholars suggest that the probable time of the writing is close to the period of the Exile (598-538 B.C.).

Some scholars have questioned the historicity of the events as recorded in the book. However, there does not seem to be any substantive reason to support such a view. In fact, there are strong indications that the story as we have it is quite authentic. For example, it may be noted that King David manifested an interesting attitude of tolerance, respect and acceptance toward the Moabites as is shown in I Samuel 22:3-4 NRSV:

> David went from there to Mizpeh of Moab.
>
> He said to the king of Moab, "Please let my
>
> father and mother come to you, until I know
>
> what God will do for me." He left them with
>
> the king of Moab, and they stayed with him
>
> all the time that David was in the stronghold.

Thus, we have provided for us a literary confirmation that the great-grandmother of David was Ruth, the Moabitess. It may be that the motive of the unknown author of the Book of Ruth was simply to record something of the history of certain of David's ancestors. One factor is evident: the author succeeded in writing a beautiful, compelling and altogether interesting short story.

Note: Unless otherwise designated, the scripture quotations in this book are taken from the New Revised Standard Version Bible, copyright 1989, Division of Christian Education of the National Council of Churches in the United States of America.

CHAPTER ONE

THE JOURNEY TO MOAB

1. *In the days when the judges ruled, there was a famine in the land, and a certain man of Bethlehem of Judah went to live in the country of Moab, he and his wife and two sons.*

Bethlehem of Judah was the very center of the territory given by God in His covenant arrangement with Abraham. Therefore, it is to be designated in our story as the place of God's choosing for His people to dwell.

The event of a famine is stated in matter-of-fact manner. The point is clear that famines are not unusual experiences in that land. In fact, they are to be expected. The resident of the area, therefore, lives *through them in anticipation of inevitable change in the climate. In* other words, it is prudent to remain in the place of God's choosing in faith of His deliverance.

To re-signify this biblical principle to our own day, it remains true that "in every life some rain must fall!" The true believer refuses to lose faith in the face of expected and unexpected difficulties. Rather, the certainty of God's unfailing intervention is embraced. Such is the view of Israel's great King David:

Even though I walk through the darkest

valley,

I fear no evil;

for you are with me. . . .

Psalm 23:4

2. ***The name of the man was Elimelech (my God is King), and the name of his wife was Naomi (Pleasant One), and the names of his two sons were Mahlon (Sick One) and Chilion (Pining One); they were Ephrathites from Bethlehem in Judah. They went into the country of Moab and remained there.***

The significance of the names should not go unnoticed. The imagery becomes clear. This verse may be read accordingly: Once there lived in Judah a man known as "My God is King." The name of his wife was "Pleaant One." Their names implied the existence of a strong and compatible relationship. It was seen as the ideal marriage of a couple living in the place of God's choosing for them. However, the names by which they called their sons suggest that there is something missing. "Sick One" and "Pining One" (Could these be nicknames?) present the image of dissatisfaction and an attitude of negativity.

When discordant notes appear in the symphony of life, harmony becomes an elusive component. This is true in individual families, communities, society in general, and that includes the church as well.

Frequently, there exist groups in the church and/or individuals who, although professing Christian faith and loyalty to the church, are given to attitudes of negativity. Sadly, in such instances, it is possible for otherwise sincere Christians to evolve into oppositional factors within the congregation. Often such individuals and families elect to separate in fact or in spirit from the congregation. What is the term we use in this instance? Well, it often is referred to as "backsliding." Inevitably, such a course of action is personally debilitating and even self-destructive spiritually to the disenchanted person or group.

Our text informs us that Elimelech and his family "remained there." The point is that the backsliding condition often is permanent. When one has exercised the oppositional position by the act of leaving the circle of relationship and fellowship, it becomes likely that the attitude of defensiveness will occur, making the return to the group extremely difficult.

An abiding principle emerges: When you are in the place of God's choosing for you – stay there!

3. ***But Elimelech, the husband of Naomi, died, and she was left with her two sons.***

What a very sad development in the lives of Elimelech and Naomi! In their instance, self-determination resulted in unexpected disaster. In a strange and distant environment, Naomi was bereft of the comfort and support of family and friends. She found herself in a community of herself and her two sons, for whose food and shelter she was singularly responsible. It often has been observed that personal decision determines personal destiny. We have just learned that the personal decision of Elimelech determined the undesirable destiny of Naomi as well.

4. ***These took Moabite wives; the name of the one was Orpah (Stiff Neck) and the name of the other was Ruth (Friend or Companion).***

One of the basic tenets of the Hebrew tradition involved the importance of inner-tribal marriage. In other words, to marry outside the Hebrew tribal structure was viewed in a very negative light. This is not difficult for us to understand. After all, we are familiar with Christian parents advising their maturing children to seek friends and marriage partners within church relationships. Generally speaking, such counsel is reasonable, valid and appropriate. After all, for even the most accommodating and mutually compatible couple, marriage often is "no walk in the park" as they say. When "different" and "strange" traditions are stirred into the mix, the strains and stresses of co-existence within the family become challenging, to say the least. Within the story as we have it, there does not exist evidence of familial discord. Nevertheless, tragedy strikes!

5. *When they had lived there about ten years, both Mahlon and Chilion also died, so that the woman was left without her two sons and her husband.*

All semblance of security and family stability vanished. Naomi was confronted with the stark reality of isolation in a foreign land with the added responsibility of two daughter-in-law to further complication the issue. Such unexpected eventualities are a universal phenomenon. We all experience times of deep and personal trouble.

Indeed, we all suffer trouble, and many times there are no explanations for such trouble. Actually, the shadow of mystery which is too deep for us to comprehend looms over our existence. Yet our Christian faith affirms our suffering just as it affirms the suffering of Jesus. When we experience tears, failure, human limitation, and even death, it is well for us to remember that it is in the crucible of agony that God transforms human limitation into true greatness. Therefore, let us follow the direction provided us by the Apostle Paul: "In everything give thanks. . . "

6. *Then she started to return with her daughters-in-law from the country of Moab, for she had heard in the country of Moab that the Lord had considered his people and given them food.*

One might wonder what thoughts circulated in the mind of Naomi during those days: Why did we ever leave Judah? Why did we doubt that God would not fail to deliver His people? Did we forget or ignore our heritage as people who were delivered from slavery to freedom? Why did we fail to trust in the mercy and grace of our God? Why did it take this tragic experience to awaken me to a renewed awareness of God and His purpose for my life?

Jesus once related the story of the Prodigal Son. In that account, the young son secured from his father his portion of the father's estate, and forthwith, he proceeded to squander his inheritance in a foreign land. Finally, when at the end of his resources, he came to himself while working in the pig pen. He, too, "had to hit the bottom" before he was awakened to his pitiful plight. Like Naomi, he resolved to return home.

How altogether blessed we would be if we could but learn to seek God's will, do God's will, and trust God's purpose for our lives. An abiding principle emerges here: God has a perfect plan for every life. We need only trust and obey. In other words, determine always to remain in the place of God's choosing for us. Therein is peace, security, and happiness.

7-14 So she set out from the place where she had been living, she and her two daughters-in-law, and they went on their way to go back to the land of Judah. But Naomi said to her daughters-in-law, "Go back each of you to your mother's house. May the Lord deal kindly with you, as you have dealt with the dead and with me. The Lord grant that you may find security, each of you in the house of your husband." Then she kissed them and they wept aloud. They said to her, "No, we will return with you to your people." But Naomi said, "Turn back, my daughters, Why will you go with me? Do I have sons in my womb that they may become your husbands? Turn back, my daughters, go your way, for I am too old to have a husband. Even if I thought there were hope for me, even if I should have a husband tonight and bear sons, would you then wait until they were grown? Would you then refrain from marrying? No, my daughters, it has been far more bitter for me than for you, because the hand of the Lord has turned against me." Then they wept aloud again. Orpah kissed her mother-in-law, but Ruth clung to her.

There is an undesignated factor influencing the progression of this fascinating story. That phantom factor is known as the Levirate Principle. Usually known as Levirate Marriage, it is based on the directive found in the book of Deuteronomy 25:5-10. In simple terms, this refers to a situation in which the husband dies and leaves his young wife with no children. In order that the name of the dead might be preserved, the widow will be married to his next of kin, usually a surviving brother. The first-born male child of that union will bear the name of the dead. Therefore, when a young woman marries into a family, she becomes the responsibility of the family. Therefore, Naomi was heir to the responsibility of providing appropriate husbands for her daughters-in-law that the names of her sons might be preserved in Israel.

> Initially, the comments of Naomi appear as considerate, compassionate and altogether supportive to the best interests of her daughters-in-law. However, the religion and traditions of her people retained an inescapable factor which she could not escape. She had an undeniable responsibility. Nevertheless, Naomi attempted by subtle logic to dissuade Orpah and Ruth from their desire to accompany her to Judah. We may ponder the reason. Did she have a desire for personal freedom without the baggage of foreign girls to limit her own goals in life? Did the years of absence from the constant presence and influence of Jewish law and tradition result in a psychological and spiritual deadening of her personal faith and sense of belonging to the Hebrew community? Had she reached a point in life when selfishness and self-serving consumed her and abrogated the lofty virtues of compassion, generosity and benevolence?

> Perhaps there is a poignant lesson for each of us in this story. As in the case of Elimelech and Naomi, when one leaves the place and position of God's choosing for life, it becomes increasingly easy to drift into an extended posture of negligence and indifference to God, His word, and His people. To

state it differently, when one willfully goes his own way, does his own thing, and ignores God, faith and responsibility, the path toward complete narcissism is paved with selfishness and indifference to other's needs, desires and objectives.

Naomi, as a believer in the God of Abraham, Isaac and Jacob, should have pursued Ruth and Orpah and urged them to join her in the Promised Land. Rather, she urged them to return to Moab, a pagan land. Actually, it was a polite way for her to tell the girls to "go to Hell!" This line of thinking may prompt some of us to ponder our own response to persons who are not believers in Christ. After all, it is either an invitation to come with us to life with Jesus Christ, or, in whatever way we may say it, "Go to Hell!"

15-17 So she said, "See, your sister-in-law has gone back to her people and to her gods; return after your sister-in-law." But Ruth said,

> "Do not press me to leave you
>
> or to turn back from following you!
>
> Where you go, I will go;
>
> where you lodge, I will lodge;
>
> your people shall be my people,
>
> and your God my God.
>
> Where you die, I will die-
>
> there will I be buried.
>
> May the Lord do thus and so to me,

and more as well,

if even death parts me from you!"

In this exquisite ode to devotion, there is to be found principles of personal commitment which form the basis for purposive and triumphant living. In this narrative of Ruth the Moabite alien to the Jewish heritage, there is expressed her determined dedication to her mother-in-law and her people and religion. It is profoundly significant when one's relationship to a person and/or a cause is declared with sincere open-hearted resolve. This incident reflects the character of Christian discipleship. When one responds to the Savior's call to follow Him, such determined dedication and open-hearted resolve is indicative of the validity and extent of personal dedication to the Christ and His mission. The words of the familiar chorus come to mind here:

"I have decided to follow Jesus,

No turning back! No turning back!"

"Where you go, I will go; where you lodge, I will lodge." There are no territorial or geographic boundaries in the disciple's commitment to the Lord. The petition of Ruth to Naomi involved a pledge without strings attached. Such is the nature of authentic discipleship. The lines of the hymn, "I'll Go Where You Want Me to Go" express this principle with great power:

"It may not be on the mountain's height,

Or over the stormy sea;

It may not be at the battle's front

My Lord will have need of me;

But if by a still small voice He calls

> To paths I do not know,
>
> I'll answer, dear Lord, with my hand in Thine,
>
> I'll go where you want me to go.
>
> I'll go were you want me to go, dear Lord,
>
> O'er mountain, or plain, or sea;
>
> I'll say what you want me to say, dear Lord,
>
> I'll be what you want me to be."

Ruth's stated desire to become a part of the people of God is a giant step for her in her effort truly to enter into a new and meaningful life. The principle here is pertinent to the Christian as well. As one becomes a true follower of Jesus, one soon realizes that such a decision inevitably involves becoming a part of the family of God, that is the Church. It is appropriate to question why affiliation with a particular congregation has important value for the believer. Because the Church is the visible manifestation of the spiritual body of Christ, it is to be respected, supported, and loved. It is where the truth of God and His redemptive provision in Jesus Christ is taught, and where fellowship with the Lord and His own people is shared. Ultimately, it is in, with, and for the Church that the mission of Christ is best actualized on earth. Indeed, it is a grand and transcendent benefit to the believer who rejoices in the reality of being a part of the family of God.

Ruth insists that her commitment to Naomi is binding and permanent. She insists that she will remain in Judah and die and a be buried alongside of Naomi.

She then summarized that nothing, not even death, will be able to separate them. Again, this is the level of devotion each Christian should affirm in personal loyalty, love, and service. Further, it is appropriate in other aspects of life as well. It is ideal as a worthy objective in marriage. The principle of permanence solidifies the marriage relationship, strengthens the complete family structure, and contributes to the quality of society as a whole.

18, 19 *When Naomi saw that she was determined to go with her, she said no more to her.*

So the two of them went on until they came to Bethlehem. When they came to Bethlehem, the whole town was stirred because of them;

"Is this Naomi?"

The reception given Naomi and Ruth by the Bethlehem community is quite interesting. To state it in plain talk, the town got excited over the return of Naomi and the arrival of Ruth. What an unexpected homecoming for Naomi! No resentment toward her for her previous decision to leave them! No expressed skepticism pertaining to her possible motives in returning! No evidence of resistance to her bringing a Moabite woman with her! Rather, there was genuine joy among the people to have a beloved neighbor and friend come home.

But what about the reception for Ruth? She was no returning citizen of Bethlehem. Indeed, she was not from Israel at all. In fact, as we might say it today, she was an undocumented alien. Nevertheless, the family and friends of Naomi were excited about the advent of Ruth, just as they were over the return of her mother-in-law. Perhaps word of her kindness toward Naomi had preceded her. Or, it may have been pleasing to them that one so young and attractive as Ruth would seek to become one of them. Certainly we may be confident that Ruth's relationship with Naomi was a contributing factor to the joy of the villagers over her arrival.

For the moment, allow the image of the Bethlehem citizens to represent the church in your town or community. There are two events certain to bring joy to any congregation. One is the sight of a "backslider" returning home to the life of the church and its fellowship. Another is the sight of a person coming to faith in Jesus Christ as Savior and Lord. These experiences, individually or collectively, inevitably serve as prelude to spiritual revival in the life of the church.

20, 21 She said to them, "Call me no longer Naomi, call me Mara, for the Almighty hath deat bitterly with me. I went away full, but the Lord has brought me back empty.

Previous to the receiving of the full benefits of the love and fellowship of her family and friends, Naomi expressed true regret for her present plight in life. Again, an unavoidable principle of the redemptive process emerges. The awareness, acceptance, and confession of personal sin is essential to the cleansing of the spirit. Then it becomes possible to experience the grace of love, peace, and fellowship.

Again, in simple terms, we may ponder how one goes about the process of true repentance. Actually, the process is clear so that all persons, regardless of education or estate in life, can understand and experience the repentance needed.

1. LOOK AT YOURSELF! This will not be easy, but do it anyway. So, you have done wrong! Perhaps you are disgusted with yourself! You are unhappy with yourself as you are. Really, you would like to return home. Well, you can, and here is how.
2. TRUST IN GOD. God is love. If I truly understand love, it is synonymous with grace and forgiveness. You

often hear others speak of receiving God's love. If He loves others, He certainly loves you as well.

3. DO SOMETHING ABOUT IT! Once again, we return to the account in which Jesus tells the story involving the Prodigal Son. Remember that the Prodigal Son did not just remain sitting in the swine pen and reflect on home with a choking nostalgia. He did not just squat in his squalor and murmur a prayer for God's help. He got up and started home! So, do something about yourself. Reflect! Repent! Then start home! God waits to welcome you back!

22 So Naomi returned together with Ruth, the Moabite, her daughter-in-law, who came back with her from the country of Moab. They came to Bethlehem at the beginning of barle harvest.

Chapter one of the book begins with a famine and it ends with a harvest. The lesson for us is quite clear. The trials and troubles of life are universal, and they come to all people, even the people of God. Christians do suffer illness, sorrow, financial difficulty, familial stress, and conflict from many sources. Always, there exists the temptation to run from the scene. However, God does not forsake his people, and the time of blessing is certain to return. Therefore, the believer will stay in the place of God's choosing for his life, always trusting in God who never forsakes us.

CHAPTER TWO

GLEANING IN THE FIELDS

1. *Now Naomi had a kinsman on her husband's side, a prominent rich man, of the family of Elimelech, whose name was Boaz.*

We are now introduced to the "kinsman-redeemer" who is destined to play the primary role in the establishing of Ruth as a member of the family of Elimelech. The Hebrew root of the name Boaz, means "He will establish." In every way, in his relationship with Ruth, Boaz fulfills the true meaning of his name. He is her savior, delivering her from a life of obscurity and insignificance to a life of meaning, relationship, and purpose.

It is easy to see how Boaz is a type of Jesus Christ! Like Boaz, Jesus is our kinsman-redeemer. It is Jesus who enters into our lives and delivers us from sin, insecurity, and hopelessness. It is Jesus who, by His sacrifice on the cross, pays the price of our redemption, and establishes us as members of the family of God in which we realize meaning, relationship, and purpose. May God help us to respond to Jesus, as Ruth responded to Boaz, with obedience and love.

2. *And Ruth the Moabite said to Naomi, "Let me go to the field and glean among the ears of grain, behind someone in whose sight I may find favor." She said to her, "Go, my daughter."*

A very important phenomenon developed in the mind and heart of Ruth. There existed a strong desire to experience the kind and quality of faith and life which she was witnessing in Naomi and her family and friends. There was something about the faith expressions of the Jewish people that surpassed anything she had known before. She desired to know more about the matter, so she was willing to place herself in a position to realize her desires.

This fact introduces a universal principle which is pertinent to each of us. Inherent within us is a longing to know God and experience a relationship with Him. It has been said that there exists in us a God-shaped space which only God can fill. If we but realized it, we never know true peace until we satisfy that longing for God. Ruth is a worthy example for us to immulate. She gave redemptive action to her desire. We do well to take the same approach. If we do take such action, we shall be rewarded with the desire of our heart.

3. *So she went. She came and gleaned in the field behind the reapers. As it HAPPENED, she came to the part of the field belonging to Boaz, who was of the family of Elimelech.*

Central to understanding this verse is that word, "happened." In the contemporary vernacular, we associate this word with the idea of chance. In the ancient Hebrew sensibility, nothing could be farther from the truth. We might better translate the passage as "it was her DESTINY to light in the field belonging to Boaz. Specifically, the idea here is the role of the providence of God in the affairs of humankind.

Paul writes, "...all things work together for good..."(Romans 8:28). Most of us believe that this is a true statement. Yet when we are struggling in the difficult situations of life, sometimes we find ourselves doubting the idea that God is working for our good. Then we get down on ourselves for doubting, and our misery is intensified.

Two observations regarding this matter may prove to have value. First, do not be concerned about your doubts. You do not believe your doubts, therefore, they do not matter. Secondly, continue to affirm what you believe. Regardless of your occasional doubts, you remain convinced that God indeed is working for your good in everything. Out task is to learn to trust the purpose of God. After all, we do believe!

See! It was not by chance that Ruth found herself gleaning in the field that belonged to Boaz. She was there by divine appointment. God was working for her good, as we shall see.

4. ***Just then Boaz came from Bethlehem. He said to the reapers, "The Lord be with you." They answered, "The Lord bless you."***

> At casual reading, this verse seems to record a gracious, courteous, and quite socially polite exchange of greetings between Boaz and his employees. As a matter of fact, it was exactly that. Yet there is more here that will prove relevant and instructive for our time as well.
>
> The fundamental principle for effective management and labor relationship is presented in this brief formula. Boaz (management) approached the reapers (labor) with a reverent invocation of divine intervention in their interest and behalf. The impression is evident that the essential interest of Boaz was not the financial profit of the enterprise. In other words, his efforts were person centered, not the accumulating assets of his corporate balance sheet.

The response of the reapers to Boaz was no less impressive. They, too, petitioned the Lord to bless their employer. The entire exchanged greetings portray the ideal system in which all persons involved realized the personal and group value of mutual respect. Surely we can realize that this is a spiritually and economically feasible arrangement which retains integrity and compatibility for both sides. Our current news is filled constantly with conflict and even legal disputation between management and labor. May God help us to realize that the solution to such issues is to be found in the simple and elemental principles of corporate and individual mutual affirmation and respect. For the sake of the nation and future generations, please, God, help us to get back to the Word of God for faith and practice.

5-7 Then Boaz said to his servant who was in charge of the reapers, "To whom does this young woman belong?" The servant who was in charge of the reapers answered, "She is the Moabite who came back with Naomi from the country of Moab. She said, 'Please let me glean and gather among the sheaves behind the reapers.' So she came, and she has been on her feet from early this morning until now, without resting even for a moment."

Already we have learned of Boaz's interest and concern for those persons who were in his employ. Of course, the reapers were Jews. Now, we discover that Boaz takes an interest in a person who is not Jewish Ruth is a Moabite. To state it differently, she was a Gentile. Increasingly it is clear that Boaz, for the sake of this study, is a type of Christ. Therefore, it is no surprise to discover in him a concern and personal interest in all persons, Jew and Gentile.

Immediately, the thoughts of the Christian return to the mission directive of our Lord Jesus: "Go therefore and make disciples of ALL NATIONS, baptizing them in the name of the Father and of the Son and of the Holy Spirit, and teaching them to obey everything that I have commanded you. And remember, I am with you always, to the end of the age (Matt. 28:19, 20 NRSV)."

In conclusion, the Book of Ruth reveals to us that in the true religion of the Bible, there is no provincialism or narrow sectarianism designed to exclude any person or group. Indeed, authentic Christian religion worships a universal God whose love is likewise universal. "God so loved the world (Jews and Gentiles)."

8, 9 *Then Boaz said to Ruth, "Now listen, my daughter, do not go to glean in another field or leave this one, but keep close to my young women. Keep your eyes on the field that is being reaped, and follow behind them. I have ordered the young men not to bother you. If you get thirsty, go to the vessels and drink from what the young men have drawn.*

Several golden nuggets of truth are found in the mine of these two brief verses. For one thing, there is the establishment of a relationship in Boaz's address to Ruth. He refers to her as "my daughter." These words reveal an awareness on the part of Boaz of a personal responsibility for Ruth. This principle is transcendent! Each individual in the human family has a relationship with the Almighty God. We are related to Him by the process of divine creation. Therefore, God has a responsibility for His own creation. The familiar line from John 3:16 echoes this fact: "For God so loved the world. . ."

Notice Boaz's instruction to Ruth that she "keep close to my young women. . . " It is logical to ponder this counsel. Why did he say it? What does it mean? Well, several thoughts come to mind. For one thing, Ruth is a foreigner and, therefore, unfamiliar with the Judean way of doing things. There are feminine customs, traditions and social graces common among young Jewish women, and Ruth will learn much from her association with them. Perhaps more importantly, such close involvement with the Jewish young women in their work will provide Ruth the opportunity for increased fellowship beyond her limited ties with Naomi.

It is significant to note that if Ruth follows the directive of Boaz and remains in his field, he has arranged for her security and provided for her physical need for refreshment. So what are the guarantees promised Ruth? Simply stated, they are fellowship, instruction, security, and provision. In other words, Boaz pledged to meet her every need.

The outline of God's covenant with His redeemed people (the Church, i.e. the Body of Christ) is reflected in the pledge of Boaz to Ruth. When we determine to follow Christ as true disciples, we, too, are promised fellowship, security, and provision.

10-13 Then she fell prostrate, with her face to the ground, and said to him, "Why have I found favor in your sight, that you should take notice of me, when I am a foreigner?" Boaz answered her, "All that you have done for your mother-in-law since the death of your husband has been fully told me, and how you left your father and mother and your native land and came to a people that you did not know before. May the Lord reward you for your deeds, and may you have a full reward from the Lord, the God of Israel, under whose wings you have come for refuge.

As we follow the story of Ruth, increasingly we come to respect and admire her. Therefore, it comes as a bit of surprise when she prostrated herself before Boaz and, declared her personal unworthiness for his attention, proceededed to question how he could possibly take notice of her. She was struck by the fact that he even noticed her. What an overwhelming moment this was for the young widow from Moab as she became aware that Boaz had concern for her, and exhibited it.

It is a transforming event when we Christians pause to reflect on the fact that the eternal God knows us, knows about us, and has exhibited that concern in the person of our Savior, God's Son. This awareness on our part is overwhelming for us as well. The familiar lines penned by George Beverly Shea express our amazement that God would take note of us:

There's the wonder of sunset at evening,

The wonder as sunrise I see;

But the wonder of wonders that thrills my soul

Is the wonder that God loves me.

O the wonder of it all, the wonder of it all

Just to think that God loves me!

O the wonder of it all, the wonder of it all –

Just to think that God loves me!

14-16 *At meantime Boaz said to her, "Come here and eat some of this bread, and dip your morsel in the sour wine." So she sat beside the reapers, and he heaped up for her some parched grain. She ate until she was satisfied, and she had some left over. When she got up to glean, Boaz instructed his young men, "Let her glean even among the standing sheaves, and do not reproach her. You must also pull out some handfuls for her from the bundles, and leave them for her to glean, and do not rebuke her."*

As one carefully reads this passage, it may be noted that there are at least two factors of significance which should be considered. In the first place, there is the account of Boaz serving bread and wine to Ruth. There is about this event a sacramental implication. Recall that as Christians observe the Eucharist (Lord's Supper), there is the remembering the sacrifice of Jesus on the cross for our salvation. In addition, there also is inherent in the experience the anticipation of the great heavenly banquet to be shared with our Lord in Heaven. So for Ruth, there is in the giving and receiving of the bread and wine the promise of future security, provision, and fellowship.

In the second place, there is the directive by Boaz that his reapers leave "handfuls on purpose" for the benefit of Ruth. This is symbolic of a redemptive principle which is for the benefit of all God's people in their journey through life. Think of the many handfuls on purpose left in your way as you proceed along life's pathway. There are loving and caring parents, dedicated school teachers, faithful pastors and other religious leaders, the richness of great literature, and the inspiration of beautiful music. The list goes on and on. God has left abundant handfuls on purpose in our lives as we journey the path that leads us Home.

17-23 So she gleaned in the field until evening. Then she beat out what she had gleaned, and it was about an ephah of barley. She picked it up and came into the town, and her mother-in-law saw how much she had gleaned. Then she took out and gave her what was left over after she herself had been satisfied. Her mother-in-law said to her, "Where did you glean today? And where have you worked? Blessed be the man who took notice of you." So she told her mother-in-law with whom she had worked, and said, "The name of the man with whom I worked today is Boaz." Then Naomi said to her daughter-in-law, "Blessed be he by the Lord, whose kindness has not forsaken the living or the dead!" Naomi also said to her, "The man is a relative of ours, one of our nearest kin." Then Ruth the Moabite said, "He even said to me, 'Stay close to my servants, until they have finished all my harvest.'" Naomi said to Ruth, her daughter-in-law, "It is better, my daughter, that you go out with his young women, otherwise you might be bothered in another field." So she stayed close to the young women of Boaz, gleaning until the end of the barley and wheat harvest; and she lived with her mother-in-law.

Several components of authentic religious living emerge in these verses. These components are easily identified in Christian discipleship as well. They include at least the following:

1. In the diligent and faithful work of Ruth, work that continues in the field throughout the day, one may realize the sanctity of common labor. As the work of Ruth was noted by Boaz, we are convinced that the daily tasks of our own lives are within the concern of God.

2. At the conclusion of her day of labor, Ruth is seen sharing the fruits of that labor with Naomi. The key word here is "sharing." As we recall the story of the early Christians as given in the Book of Acts, it is recorded that a basic characteristic was their sharing all things together. Through the centuries, the qualities of munificence, compassion and social action have remained a constant in the history of the Church.

3. Religious education emerges in the relationship between Ruth and her mother-in-law, Naomi. The latter takes the time to instruct Ruth on the principle and purpose of the "near-kinsman" law. As a result of these moments of teaching, Ruth is able to proceed in her quest for a permanent relationship with Boaz. Clearly, religious education has remained primary among Christians of all generations. This is evident in all levels of endeavor, from Sunday School classes in local congregations to colleges and universities throughout the world.

4. The last sentence of this passage provides a very significant clue to meaningful religious living. "She continued living with her mother-in-law." To grow as a Christian, we will do well to stay close to other believers. Fellowship provides us with comfort, protection, and encouragement.

CHAPTER THREE

RUTH AND BOAZ AND THE NIGHT AT THE THRESHING FLOOR

The threshing floor scene which dominates chapter three involves a practice that is unique to that time and place. When the harvest of the grain was complete and stored in great piles on the designated ground, it was necessary for the land-owner to remain in camp on the spot. Otherwise, thieves would steal the grain during the night, and the livelihood of the proprietor would be taken from him. Further, it was standard operating procedure for the servants and other contract employees to remain with the proprietor through the night. With this familiar arrangement, any needs of the owner which might arise during the night could be attended efficiently and immediately. It was this precise situation which found Ruth present and prepared to render attention to any issue involving the needs of Boaz.

1-5 Naomi her mother-in-law said to her, "My daughter, I need to seek some security for you, so that it may be well with you. Now here is our kinsman Boaz, with whose young women you have been working. See, he is winnowing Barley tonight at the threshing floor. Now WASH yourself and ANOINT yourself, and PUT ON YOUR BEST CLOTHES and go down to the threshing floor; but DO NOT MAKE YOURSELF KNOWN TO THE MAN until he has finished eating and drinking. When he lies down, observe the place where he lies; then go and uncover his feet and lie down; and he will tell you what to do." She said to her, "All that you tell me I will do."

At last, the reluctant Naomi began to actualize her legal responsibility of securing a husband for Ruth. Perhaps her return to Judah and regular religious activity with family and friends served to revive in her an appreciation of her responsibility. At any rate, with an adroit precision, Naomi outlined for Ruth the exact manner in which she should proceed to acquire the attention of Boaz. There is a fitting lesson here for each of us: Mature Christians should take every opportunity to dialogue, counsel and encourage younger believers. All too often, we are reluctant warriors in the service of our Lord.

In biblical symbolism, night is often representative of the reality of death. Therefore, the directives of Naomi to Ruth regarding her preparation for the night on the threshing floor are implicatory of one's personal preparation for death. Ruth was advised to WASH herself, ANOINT herself, and PUT ON HER BEST CLOTHES. In symbol, we are provided here the biblical plan for salvation:

1. In our preparation to pass through the portals of death into the presence of God, we must be cleansed from our sin. When one experiences the saving cleansing of God, the joy of the soul knows no bounds:

   > I'm so glad I'm a part of the family of God,
   >
   > I've been washed in the fountain,
   >
   > Cleansed by his blood.
   >
   > - Gaither

2. The experience of anointing suggests the realization of the presence and power of the Living God within us and upon us to accomplish His purpose in our lives. We are reminded here of the special anointing of our Lord:

   > And when Jesus had been baptized, just as he came up from the water, suddenly the heavens were opened to him and he saw the Spirit of God descending like a dove and alighting on him. And a voice from heaven said, "This is my Son, the

beloved, with whom I am well pleased. -Matthew 3:16, 17.

Indeed, it as we embrace the anointing of the Spirit in our lives that we are truly prepared to face the inevitable issues of life, including the reality of our own mortality.

3. With the phrase, "Put on your best clothes," we are introduced to the idea of sanctification. For Christians, this refers to our becoming more and more like Christ, ever looking forward to our standing in His presence in Heaven where we shall "be like Him." That is sanctification perfected.

6-13 So she went down to the threshing floor and did just as her mother-in-law had instructed her. When Boaz had eaten and drunk and he was in a contented mood, he went to lie down at the end of the heap of grain. Then she came stealthily and uncovered his feet, and lay down. At midnight the man was startled, and turned over, and there, lying at his feet, was a woman! He said, "Who are you?" And she answered, "I am Ruth, your servant; spread your cloak over your servant, for you are next of kin." He said, "May you be blessed by the Lord, my daughter; this last instance of your loyalty is better than the first; you have not gone after young men; whether poor or rich. And now, my daughter, do not be afraid, I will do for you all that you ask, for all the assembly of my people know that you are a worthy woman. But now, though it is true that I am a near kinsman, there is another kinsman more closely related than I. Remember this night, and in the morning, if he will act as next-of-kin for you, good; let him do it. If he

is not willing to act as next-of-kin for you, then, as the Lord lives, I will act as next-of-kin for you. Lie down until the morning.

It is interesting to note at the outset of this paragraph that Ruth followed the directions of Naomi in detail. She attempted no short-cut in her effort to secure the favor of Boaz. In that setting, Boaz was her salvation. The principle is evident: There are no short-cuts in God's redemption design. There is one certain path that leads us to God, and that path is belief in the Lord Jesus Christ. Certainly, Jesus said it best, "I am the way, and the truth, and the life." Often it has been stated that without the way, there is no going; without the truth, there is no knowing; and without the life, there is no living. Indeed, Jesus is God's precise plan for our salvation.

As previously indicated, Ruth's taking her place at the feet of Boaz was not an inappropriate act on her part. Rather, she was fulfilling the role of an obedient servant, ready and willing to respond to the wishes and needs of the master.

Upon his awaking, Ruth made a request of Boaz: "Spread your cloak over your servant." Accordingly, sheltered from the chill of the night and secure in his presence, she was prepared for the darkness of the night.

In symbol, we have a picture of the Christian facing the inevitable experience of death, covered in the righteousness of our Lord Jesus Christ. As in the instance of Ruth, we "rest in peace" secure in the presence of our Redeemer. We recall the beloved words of King David"

> Even though I walk through the darkest valley,
>
> I fear no evil;
>
> for you are with me;

your rod and your staff –

they comfort me . . .

Psalm 23:4

Boaz was careful to remind Ruth of a fact which she might easily have forgotten, or, perhaps, had never realized. Boaz stated that there was another near kinsman in the family who was nearer kin to her than he was. He then pledged to confront and deal with the other near kinsman in behanl of Ruth. We are reminded that while Jesus became man, and, therefore, is as we are, there is one more like us than He. Jesus was sinless. We are sinners. In our sinful nature, we are nearer Satan than we are Jesus. However, we have the pledge that Jesus will settle the matter of our sinful nature. Therefore, the death, burial, and resurrection of Jesus is the ultimate solving of our sin problem. And what are we to do? Believe on the Lord Jesus Christ and we are safe and saved.

After assuring her that he intendeds to deal with the other near kinsman, Boaz provided Ruth with the advice that she should "Lie down until the morning." Can you imagine what thoughts Ruth entertained that night as she anticipated Boaz's intervention in her behalf? What a great day it would prove to be for her! The day would come! So she must be patient until then. We Christians also are awaiting the dawn of that eternal day in which we shall realize the fulfillment of our Lord's promise, "I will come again and receive you unto myself, that where I am, there you will be also." Perhaps Stuart Hamblen has captured the essence of our joyous anticipation:

"My heart can sing when I pause to remember

a heart-ache here is but a stepping stone –

along a trail that's winding always upward.

This troubled world is not my final home.

But until then my heart will go on singing;

Until then, with joy I'll carry on –

until the day my eyes behold the city,

until the day God calls me home."

14-18 *So she lay at his feet until morning, but got up before one person could recognize another; for he said, "It must not be known that the woman came to the threshing floor." Then he said, "Bring the cloak you are wearing and hold it out." So she held it, and he measured out six measures of barley and put it on her back; then went into the city. She came to her mother-in-law, who said, "How did things go with you, my daughter?" Then she told her all that the man had done for her, saying, "He gave me these six measures of barley, for he said, 'Do not go back to your mother-in-law empty-handed.'" She replied, "Wait, my daughter, until you learn how the matter turns out, for the man will not rest, but will settle the matter today."*

The third chapter is concluded with a very interesting event. Reference is made here to Boaz giving Ruth six measures of barley as she departed to rejoin Naomi. There is significance in the number of six. As we know, numbers had importance in Jewish sensibility and logic. For example, the number 1 meant beginning; the number 3 references deity; 5 is the number that speaks of grace; 6 represents incompleteness; and 7 is the number of completion. So, the gift of six measures of barley suggests that there is more to come. As the story unfolds, we learn that Boaz would give himself to Ruth, and that would make perfect the reward for her love, loyalty and devotion.

Let us relate this part of the narrative to the Christian's anticipation of rewards as promised by our Lord to those who love and serve Him. What are those rewards? They are the crowns pledged to the believers:

1. The imperishable crown, 1 Corinthians 9:25

Athletes exercise self-control in all things; they do it to receive a perishable crown, but we an imperishable one.

2. The crown of rejoicing, 1 Thessalonians 2:19

For what is our hope or joy or crown of rejoicing before our Lord Jesus at His coming?

3. The crown of life, James 1:12

Blessed is anyone who endures temptation. Such a one has stood the test and will receive the crown of life that the Lord has promised to those who love Him.

4. The crown of glory, 1 Peter 5:4

And when the chief shepherd appears, you will win the crown of glory that never fades away.

5. The crown of righteousness, 2 Timothy 4:8

From now on there is reserved for me the crown of righteousness, which the Lord, the righteous judge will give me on that day, and not only to me but also to all who have longed for his appearing.

6. The reward of the Heavenly Home

7. The presence of Jesus Himself

CHAPTER FOUR

THE MARRIAGE OF BOAZ AND RUTH

1. *No sooner had Boaz gone up to the gate and sat down there than the next of kin, of whom Boaz had spoken, came passing by. So Boaz said, "Come over, friend; sit down here. And he went over and sat down.*

Immediately, there emerges in this verse the universal law of opposition. Simply stated, the natural order of things exists in the tension between positives and negatives. In the spiritual realm, there is the perennial presence of good and evil. In the story of Ruth, Boaz epitomizes the positive, the good. The other "next of kin" represents the negative, the bad.

The alert Christian remains constantly aware of the opposing forces present and struggling to enlist his attention and consequent loyalty. In our religious sensibility, we speak of the war within us between the leading of the Spirit of God and the alluring seductions of the material order. The Apostle Paul identifies the problem and provides the solution:

> **I appeal to you therefore, brothers and sisters, by the mercies of God, present your bodies as a living sacrifice, holy and acceptable to God, which is your spiritual worship. Do not be conformed to this world, but be transformed by the renewing of your minds, so that you may discern what is the will of God – what is good and acceptable and perfect.**
>
> **Romans 12:1. 2**

A second and equally important factor appears. Boaz did not hesitate to confront with open and honest dialogue the other "near kinsman." This calls to mind the remarkable encounter between Jesus and Satan that took place immediately following

His baptism (Matthew 4:1-11). In that memorable event, Jesus was presented with those worldly enticements common to us all. Satan attempted to seduce Him with the offerings of materialism, secularism and power. The responses of Jesus to the respective proposals tech us how we may resist and overcome those negative impulses. Simple! In each instance, Jesus quoted from the sacred scriptures. That is the way to have victory. Depend upon and employ the power of the Word of God.

2-6 Then Boaz took ten men of the elders of the city, and said, "Sit down here"; so they sat down. He then said to the next-of-kin, "Naomi, who has come back from the country of Moab, is selling the parcel of land that belonged to our kinsman Elimelech. So I thought I would tell you of it, and say: Buy it in the presence of those sitting here, and in the presence of the elders of my people. If you will redeem it, redeem it; but if you will not, tell me, so that I may know; for there is no one prior to you to redeem it, and I come after you." So he said, "I will redeem it." Then Boaz said, "The day you acquire the field from the hand of Naomi, you are also acquiring Ruth the Moabite, the widow of the dead man, to maintain the dead man's name on his inheritance." At this, the next-of-kin said, "I cannot redeem it for myself without damaging my own inheritance. Take my right of redemption yourself, for I cannot redeem it."

What is the role of the ten men of the elders of the city? In this regard, a central principle of the redemption process is revealed: The event of redemption is not a private matter. That which Boaz is about to accomplish for Ruth will be actualized in the open as a witness of his love for her and his adherence to the prevailing laws of the Torah. Through the years to follow, this bold intervention on the part of Boaz will be recalled with national and religious affirmation.

In an infinitely greater way, Jesus intervened in behalf of the entire human race. Further, His commitment to our redemption was in the open and altogether public. The Gospel of Matthew records the initiation of the process:

> **When morning came, all the chief priests and elders of the people conferred together against Jesus in order to bring about His death. They bound Him, led Him away, and handed Him over to Pilate, the governor (27:1,2).**

As the narrative goes, Boaz immediately confronted the other "near kinsman." In clear and unmistakable language, the stipulations of the redemption process were articulated. There were two distinct components to the requirements. In the first instance, Boaz pointed out that the person desiring to assume the responsibility of Elimelech's estate must purchase the land owned by Naomi, the widow. Such a material possession was a pleasant possibility to the near-kinsman. So he quickly responded, "I will redeem it."

Then came the second component of the contract: The man who acquired the field from Nami must also acquire Ruth the Moabite, the widow of the dead man, to maintain the dead man's name on his inheritance. Suddenly, the situation was changed, and the near-kinsman withdrew his bid. He had a great interest in adding to his material possessions, but had no interest at all in the care and support of another person. This is to say that he had no interest at all in the redemption of Ruth. His final words were, "I cannot redeem it."

The Christian religion celebrates the transcendent reality that is implied in the action of Boaz, the true Redeemer-kinsman. The concern of God is universal, including the entire created order, and that concern is focused on the human race. Surely the Gospel of John says it most clearly:

> **For God so loved the world that He gave His only Son, so that everyone who believes in Him may not perish but have eternal life (3:16).**

When the reality of this transaction is appropriated in the mind and heart of a person, the joy one feels is indescribable! Philip Bliss wrote the words that reveal the grateful heart of the believer:

> *I will sing of my redeemer*
>
> *And His wondrous love to me;*
>
> *On the cruel cross He suffered*
>
> *from the curse to set me free.*
>
> *'Sing, O sing of my Redeemer,*
>
> *with His blood He purchased me;*
>
> *on the cross He sealed my pardon,*
>
> *paid the debt and made me free.*

7 Now this was the custom in former times in Israel concerning redeeming and exchanging: to confirm a transaction, the one took off a sandal and gave it to the other; this was the manner of attesting in Israel.

There is recorded here an incident that is quite unusual, to say the least. It is the only such reference in the entire Bible. Therefore, it seems appropriate to take a close look at it. Since there is no mention of the "shoe law" found in the Mosaic laws and regulations, it is likely that this practice is pre-Deuteronomic codification. One may wonder why the unknown author of the Book of Ruth elected to include such a primitive practice. Perhaps the writer possessed a personal interest in the ancient origins of tribal customs and traditions. Of course, since there does not exist textual evidence of any sort, any notion in this regard is purely speculative. At any rate, we may be pleased that this strange incident is included in the story because it serves to enlarge our own understanding of the nature of "legal" relationships in pre-historic times.

8-12 *So when the next-of-kin said to Boaz, "acquire it for yourself," he took off his sandal. Then Boaz said to the elders and all the people, "Today you are witnesses that I have acquired from the hand of Naomi all that belonged to Elimelech and that belonged to Chilion and Mahlon. I have also acquired Ruth the Moabite, the wife of Mahlon, to be my wife, to maintain the dead man's name on his inheritance, in order that the dead man may not be cut off from his kindred and the gate of his native place; today you are witnesses." Then all the people who were at the gate, along with the elders, said, "We are witnesses. May the Lord make the woman who is coming into your house like Rachel and Leah, who together built up the house of Israel. May you produce children in Ephrathah and bestow a name in Bethlehem; and, through the children that the Lord will give you by this young woman, may your house be like the house of Perez, whom Tamar bore to Judah."*

With the redemption of Ruth settled, the witnesses and the elders were quick to affirm the arrangement. The law as given in the Torah had been honored. Further, we may be certain that the sight of one of the outstanding citizens of the community and the young widow was pleasant. Best wishes and verbalized blessings were bestowed on Boaz and his bride. It is evident that respect for their religion and traditions was inherently present within their society.

There is a significant lesson for our own day and generation: Religious faith and social mores remain unifying and preserving factors in society. We do well to embrace laws which support our faith and traditions. In the face of ideas and practices which challenge and abrogate our faith and practice, Christians must be knowledgeable and vigilant if we are to remain a moral and ethical people. Therefore, let us always celebrate the actualizing in the lives of people those virtues which we hold dear.

13 Boaz took Ruth to be his wife. When they came together, the Lord made her conceive, and she bore a son.

This is one of the most important verses pertaining to the origin of human life. It is written that "The Lord made her conceive." This is a clear statement that the conception event is a continuance of the creation process. Indeed, the beginning of the Book of Genesis might well read, "In the beginning, the Lord creates. . . " (Notice the continuous action verb in this paraphrase.) Thus, the Christian position should be that all human life is divine in origin, and, therefore, is precious to God, and should be to us as well. In the social and political realms, this conviction is often lost to a view that the abortion of the fetus is subject to the wishes of the woman involved. The person who desires any sort of biblical support for such a point of view finds zero support in the sacred scriptures. Again, this verse is relevant to these times.

14-17 Then the women said to Naomi, "Blessed be the Lord who has not left you this day without next-of-kin; and

may his name be renowned in Israel! He shall be to you a restorer of life and nourisher of your old age; for your daughter-in-law who loves you, who is more to you than seven sons, has born him. Then Naomi took the child and laid him in her bosom, and became his nurse. The women of the neighborhood gave him a name, saying, "A son has been born to Noami." They named him Obed; he became the father of Jesse, the father of David.

These verses read very much like a card of congratulations which might be sent to parents or grandparents of a new-born infant. While the birth of a baby is a particularly intimate event in the life of its parents, it also is a cause of celebration and expressions of good will from the community at large. After all, advent of the infant is an assurance of the continuity of the tribe, the community, and, indeed, the world.

Again, there emerges here a principle of pertinence to any generation, especially our own. The public affirmation of the meaning and significance of human conception, birth and life is emphasized and affirmed. Such response reflects public respect for the purpose and objective of God in the human experience.

18-20 *Now these are the descendants of Perez: Perez became the father of Hezron, Hezron of Ram, Ram of Amminadab, , Amminadab of of Nahshon, Nahshan of Salmon, Salman of Boaz, Boaz of Jesse, and Jesse of David.*

The beautiful story of Ruth is concluded with a paragraph detailing an extended genealogy of the great King David. We may speculate that the author of the book desired to demonstrate the prestige of the family into which Ruth was initiated. There is no mistaking the eminent status of the family line, culminating, of course, with Israel's greatest king.

But wait for one moment! The greatest fact regarding Ruth is found in the Gospel of Matthew, where it is revealed that she is related in the genealogy of the King of Kings, even Jesus Christ our Lord. In verses 2-16 of chapter one, there is recorded a lengthy listing of the genealogy of Jesus. It begins with Abraham and concludes with Joseph. In between are the names of the "greats" in the history of Israel, including Abraham, Isaac, Jacob, and David. Then there is included two names of unique status, both women: Rahab (of stained reputation) and Ruth (the non-Jewish Gentile). Also included is an extensive list of little-know individuals. The following verses serve to summarize the process:

> *. . . and Salmon the father of Boaz by Rahab, and Boaz the father of Obed by Ruth, and Obed the father of Jesse, and Jesse the father of King David (4:5).*

> *. . . and Jacob the father of Joseph the husband of Mary, of whom Jesus was born, who is called the Messiah (4:16).*

> *. . . She will bear a son, and you are to name him Jesus, for he will save his people from their sins (4:21).*

We close our study of the Book of Ruth with great appreciation for the wonderful story of redemption found in the Old Testament. It is a splendid prelude to the transcendent story, "the greatest story ever told," of the great Redeemer, our Lord Jesus Christ.

ACKNOWLEDGMENTS

This book is a response to many requests which I have received over the years to publish my lectures and guided studies of the Book of Ruth. Actually, this series has been the one most frequently affirmed by congregations, Sunday School classes, and special Bible Study groups. I am most grateful for the encouragement which has been extended me by individuals and classes. It is rewarding to realize that this little book, The Book of Ruth, continues to provide instruction, inspiration, profoundly significant religious formations for the Judeo-Christian community.

While affirming the never-failing support of my wife and children in each of my respective endeavors, it is appropriate to make mention of one special Sunday School Class. The Wesley Bible Class of the First United Methodist Church of Fort Worth, Texas has requested and endured our collective journey through the Book of Ruth on two occasions during the past six years. Therefore, a huge word of gratitude is extended to them.

The Book of Ruth is composed of four brief chapters. However, those chapters are rich in historical background, cultural traditions and customs, and evolving religious laws and practices. The publication of any book, even a relatively brief one, involves the participation of several professional influences. In regard to the present effort, I wish to thank in particular Abraham Caine and Christopher Sammon of the PageTurner Press for their counsel, patience and persistent encouragement.

CLH, Jr.

CPSIA information can be obtained
at www.ICGtesting.com
Printed in the USA
JSHW052322130920
7841JS00002B/96